READING CORNER

PHONICS

Blackbeard's Treasure

Written by
Sue Graves

Illustrated by
Neil Chapman

Practising long vowel phonemes,
trisyllabic words and tricky words

First published in 2010 by
Franklin Watts
338 Euston Road
London NW1 3BH

Franklin Watts Australia
Hachette Children's Books
Level 17/207 Kent Street
Sydney NSW 2000

Text © Sue Graves 2010
Illustration © Neil Chapman 2010

A CIP catalogue record for this book
is available from the British Library.

ISBN: 978 0 7496 9173 8 (hbk)
ISBN: 978 0 7496 9182 0 (pbk)

Series Editor: Jackie Hamley
Series Advisors: Dr Barrie Wade,
 Dr Hilary Minns
Series Designer: Jonathan Hair

Printed in China

Franklin Watts is a division of
Hachette Children's Books,
an Hachette UK company
www.hachette.co.uk

There is a puzzle at the end of this book.
Here are the answers for you to check later!

The matching words are:
beard cheered, feared, weird
treasure leisure, measure, pleasure
pearl curl, girl, hurl
money funny, honey, sunny

2

Blackbeard was happy.
"I'm happy because I'm
so rich," he said.

He looked in his treasure chest.

It was full of treasure.

5

There were sacks of money.

There were pots of gold.

One day, Blackbeard put too much treasure in the chest!

The ship sank a little.

Some water came in!

At first, the water came up to his feet.

15

Then the ship sank some more!
The water came up to his knees.
"Help! I'm sinking!" he cried.

17

He tried to pump out the water.

But it was no good.

19

"Oh dear," he said. "I will have to ditch my treasure in the sea. If I don't, my ship will go down!"

Splash! He threw the sacks of money in the sea.

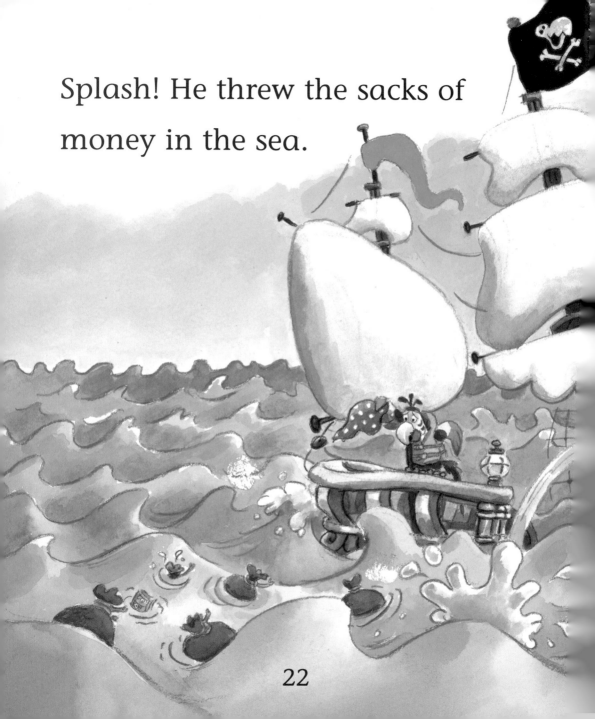

The ship came up a little.

Splash! He threw the pots
of gold in the sea.

The ship came up a little more.

Splash! He threw the bowls
of pearls in the sea.

26

The ship came up to the top of the water again.

"It was nice to have so much treasure," said Blackbeard. "But it's so much better to have my ship!"

29

Puzzle Time!

Match the words that rhyme
to the pictures.

beard

measure

curl

honey

feared

sunny

hurl

treasure

pearl

leisure

weird

funny

cheered

money

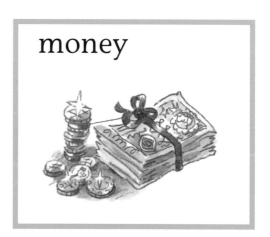

pleasure

girl

See page 2 for answers.

Notes for parents and teachers

READING CORNER PHONICS has been structured to provide maximum support for children learning to read through synthetic phonics. The stories are designed for independent reading but may also be used by adults for sharing with young children.

The teaching of early reading through synthetic phonics focuses on the 44 sounds in the English language, and how these sounds correspond to their written form in the 26 letters of the alphabet. Carefully controlled vocabulary makes these books accessible for children at different stages of phonics teaching, progressing from simple CVC (consonant-vowel-consonant) words such as "top" (t-o-p) to trisyllabic words such as "messenger" (mess-en-ger). READING CORNER PHONICS allows children to read words in context, and also provides visual clues and repetition to further support their reading. These books will help develop the all important confidence in the new reader, and encourage a love of reading that will last a lifetime!

If you are reading this book with a child, here are a few tips:

1. Talk about the story before you start reading. Look at the cover and the title. What might the story be about? Why might the child like it?

2. Encourage the child to reread the story, and to retell the story in their own words, using the illustrations to remind them what has happened.

3. Discuss the story and see if the child can relate it to their own experience, or perhaps compare it to another story they know.

4. Give praise! Small mistakes need not always be corrected. If a child is stuck on a word, ask them to try and sound it out and then blend it together again, or model this yourself. For example "wish" w-i-sh "wish".

READING CORNER PHONICS covers two grades of synthetic phonics teaching, with three levels at each grade. Each level has a certain number of words per story, indicated by the number of bars on the spine of the book:

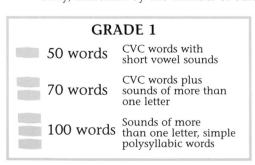

GRADE 1

	50 words	CVC words with short vowel sounds
	70 words	CVC words plus sounds of more than one letter
	100 words	Sounds of more than one letter, simple polysyllabic words

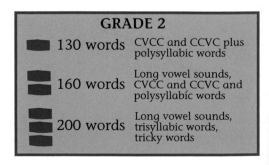

GRADE 2

	130 words	CVCC and CCVC plus polysyllabic words
	160 words	Long vowel sounds, CVCC and CCVC and polysyllabic words
	200 words	Long vowel sounds, trisyllabic words, tricky words